The Very Best Gift

Written by
Anne Palmer

Illustrated by
Lauren Faraino

THE P3 PRESS

The Very Best Gift

Printed in China through Four Colour Print Group
CPSIA Tracking Label: Printing Plant Location: Printed by Everbest Printing Co. Ltd.,
Nansha, China
Production Date: 09/01/10
Job / Batch #: 91844

For information please contact:

The P3 Press
16200 North Dallas Parkway, Suite 170
Dallas, Texas 75248
www.theP3Press.com
(972) 381-0009

A New Era in Publishing

ISBN-13: 978-1-933651-72-9
ISBN-10: 1-933651-72-5
LCCN: 2010912835

Author contact information:
theverybestgift@gmail.com

To all the people who have
The Very Best Gift and give it
away, including those whose lives
and joy inspired this book.

About the Author

Anne Palmer teaches in Birmingham, Alabama, where she lives with her adopted daughter. She is actively involved in several different types of service and mentoring projects throughout the city and hopes to continue both in teaching and in service in the future.

About the Illustrator

Lauren Faraino was born with arthrogryposis, which means she cannot use her arms, but from a young age she has loved to use her imagination. Her favorite form of expression has always been art, especially painting, which she does by holding a paintbrush with her left foot. She also enjoys reading and working with young students who need extra help with their studies. Lauren would like to eventually become an attorney so she can help individuals better understand the legal system. She is currently a student at Harvard University in Boston, Massachusetts, and her family lives in Birmingham, Alabama.

The Very Best Gift

*S*hhhhh—do you want to know a secret? Yes? Then I have a great one to tell you.

Sometimes, around birthdays or holidays, people talk a lot about gifts—the things they want to get or the things they want to give. But a lot of them have never even heard of The Very Best Gift.

You can't hold it. You can't keep it in your pocket or on a shelf. You can't pass it around for "Show and Tell." You don't need any money to have it or give it away, and if you do have it and then give it away, then you have even more than you started with. Wow! That's a pretty neat trick! Anyone can have it and give it, and it is The Very Best Gift.

So what is it? Let's visit some people who have The Very Best Gift, and I'll bet you can figure out their secret.

This is CJ. He works with boys who need to be around nice grown-ups. He laughs a lot, and he teaches the boys about history and art and music and work and play—all sorts of things! He helps them learn and grow. They have fun learning to make friends and help each other. CJ has The Very Best Gift.

This is Betty. She listens. She listens to people who tell her what they need. She listens to people who want to help others. Then she makes sure that the people who want to help others meet the people who need help. She also smiles a lot and helps other people smile, too. Betty has The Very Best Gift.

This is Ed. He likes to build houses and play fetch with his dog. At work, he helps people stop arguing about who is right and who is wrong. He also tells funny jokes and makes people laugh. Sometimes, his jokes make people forget about being mad at each other, and they feel better after he talks with them. Ed has The Very Best Gift.

4

This is Terica. She likes to do all sorts of things. Her muscles don't always work right, and doing any kind of work makes her really tired, but she keeps trying until she succeeds. She's happy, even when she's tired, and she never uses her weak muscles as an excuse. She just figures out a way to do what she wants—especially helping other people. Terica has The Very Best Gift.

This is Susan. She comes from a country where people are very poor. She came to this country to get a good education, and she worked hard in school. She still does things to help people in her country, like helping after a big flood. She collected so many things that she almost made her own flood of food and clothes! Even when she is working very hard, she takes time to help other people. Susan has The Very Best Gift.

6

This is Ruby Sue. She's very old, but she still works hard and laughs a lot. Sometimes, she claps her hands when she laughs out loud. She tells silly stories and sings funny songs while she rocks the babies she babysits. If you ask her how she can laugh so much when things are so hard for her, she smiles and says she's just happy to be alive to help others be happy. Ruby Sue has The Very Best Gift.

This is Asok. He likes computers. He invites people to come to his house to have supper or just to play on his computers. He shows people what he knows, and he gets excited when they learn something new. He can answer just about any question you ask him about computers, but he still always wants to learn more. Asok has The Very Best Gift.

This is Yoriko. She came to a new school where she didn't know anybody, and she didn't speak their language. She didn't know much English, and some of the things she said were funny. She learned to laugh about the mistakes she made, and people liked being her friend. She worked hard in school, and now she's a doctor who helps other people. Yoriko has The Very Best Gift.

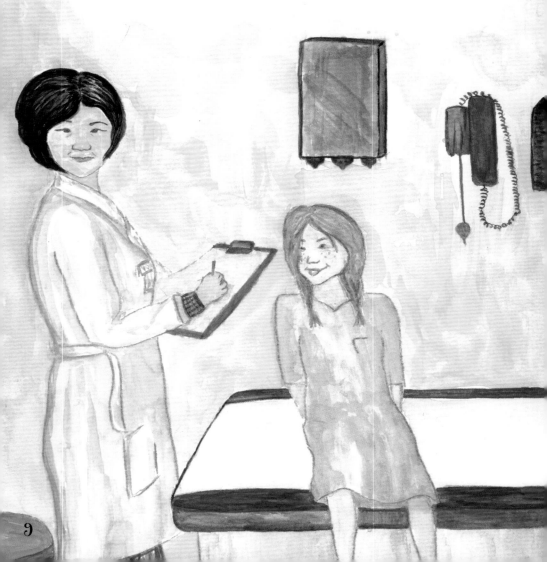

This is Madi. She has a friend in school who has a hard time reading and doing math, so Madi helps her study for tests and helps her understand things that are hard for her. She's also helping her friend figure out how to add and subtract—without even using her fingers! Madi has The Very Best Gift.

This is Reggie. His mother is very proud of him because things weren't always easy for them when he was small. He worked hard in school and became a lawyer. Now he can help other people, and his mother knows that the hard work for both of them was worth it. Reggie and his mother both have The Very Best Gift.

his is Peggy. She likes animals—dogs, cats, even
fish—and she wants to be sure that they have clean
water and a clean place to live, like people. She tells
people how to make places better and cleaner and
safer. She also tries to let others know what they can
do to help. Peggy has The Very Best Gift.

his is Stephen. He works in a church and is there every day for people who need somebody to listen to them or encourage them or cry with them. He listens, and he doesn't get mad. He tries to help people see what they can do to feel better and to be happy. Stephen has The Very Best Gift.

This is Gregory. He's not a big kid, but he helps the little kids on the playground when there's a bully around. He makes sure that the grownups know so that they can stop the bully and everybody can play together and have fun and not worry. Gregory has The Very Best Gift.

So what is The Very Best Gift? Maybe I can explain it this way: Sometimes you have something very special that you keep with you, hidden in your pocket. If it's big enough, though, everybody knows that you have something in your pocket. It shows from the inside out. That's sort of like The Very Best Gift. You can't hold it in your hand or play catch with it or put it on a shelf, but it shows from the inside out. It shows in how much you help other people. It shows when you smile. It even shows when you clean up your room without being asked. The Very Best Gift is so big that if you have it on the inside, it always shows on the outside. And the longer you have it, the bigger it gets until it shows in everything you do. That's how people know when someone has The Very Best Gift.

The secret? Not a lot of people act like they know about The Very Best Gift, but they should. It doesn't cost anything, and anyone can have it. It's the gift of love. It's the gift of spending time with your grandparents or cousins. It's the gift of listening to your mother or father or sister or brother without arguing. It's the gift of sharing toys. It's the gift of smiling when people need a smile and helping when people need help. It's the gift of loving other people just because—well, just because it makes every day a little bit better.

There's one more person I want you to see. I think this person has The Very Best Gift, but you'll have to decide for yourself. Look closely, and even if The Very Best Gift doesn't show today, it may show tomorrow or the next day. Remember how it keeps growing once a person has it. Keep looking to see if it shows. And when you look at this person, remember: The Very Best Gift is better than any gift you can buy or sell, any gift you can wrap with a ribbon, better than anything else—it's the very best in the world! And pretty soon, I think this person is going to show The Very Best Gift in a lot of different ways every day. Take a look, and see if you can see it. If you don't see it yet, keep working on it, and I'll bet it will show really soon!